Too Wild

Flash Fiction

John Sheirer

Too Wild © 2019 by John Sheirer. All rights reserved. No part of this book may be reproduced in any way without written permission from the publishers except by a reviewer who may quote brief passages to be printed in a website, newspaper, or magazine.

ISBN: 9781692113063

Many of these stories (some in different versions) have appeared in the following publications: *50 to 1; 50 Word Stories; 52/250; A Story in 100 Words; Ad Hoc Fiction; Amphibi.us; Apollo's Lyre; Back Patio Press; Big Table Publishing Website; Blake-Jones Review; Bleached Butterfly; Blink Ink; Boston Literary Magazine; Best of Boston Literary Magazine, Volume I; The Cabinet of Heed; Cautionary Tale; Best of Cautionary Tale, 2005; Clever; Daily Flash 2012; Daily Hampshire Gazette; The Drabble, Escaped Ink; Fictionesse Magazine; Flashshot; Foliate Oak; Fresh Ink; Friday Flash Fiction; Ink, Sweat, and Tears; Humor Press; Laughter Loaf; Litvision; Litsnack; Local Train Magazine; Manawaker Studios Flash Fiction Podcast; Meat for Tea; Mercurial Stories; Nights and Weekends; Obsidian River; Oddball Magazine; One-Screen Stories; Otto; Paragraph Planet; Potato Soup Journal; Pow Fast Flash Fiction; Printed Words, Raw Nervz, Rejected Manuscripts; Scarlet Leaf Review; Scribblers; Simply Pets Magazine; Six Sentences; Soft Cartel; Storyhouse; The Stray Branch; Worthing Flash; WHMP radio (Northampton, Massachusetts); Wilderness House Literary Review; Writers Resist.*

Cover photo, "Offshore Lightning Strike at Waves, North Carolina, July 2019," by John Sheirer.

SCANTIC BOOKS

https://scanticbooks.blogspot.com
Facebook: Scantic Books

Dedication

To the *Freshwater* students—
past, present, and future.

Table of Contents

8 / Keys
10 / Bad Penny
11 / Now is the Winter
12 / Loss
13 / Old Trick
14 / Yesterday's Special
16 / Command Decision
17 / Elevator
18 / Suspect
21 / How Much?
22 / How One Thing Leads to Another
23 / Motive
24 / Too Wild
26 / Curt Had a Great Deal of Anger
27 / When?
28 / TMI
32 / Breakdown Lane
33 / Third Date
34 / Christmas Eve
36 / May I Take Your Order?
37 / How We All Found Out
38 / Finish Line
39 / Frosty Walk
40 / Tough Enough
42 / Middle-Aged Man's First Text Message
43 / New
44 / The Cover-Story-Warm-Up Reader Guy
47 / Upping her Game
48 / The First Five Pages
50 / Mystery Story
51 / Somewhere Down There

52 / What to do After College
53 / Reflection
54 / Room 211
56 / No
58 / Post-Op
59 / Does this Hurt?
61 / What Kills Us
62 / Six Dreams that Might Not Be Dreams
64 / Flaws
65 / Cheat
66 / Services
67 / Mr. Boots
68 / Sunday Night
69 / Seeing Red
70 / Thirty-Nine Random, Inappropriate Thoughts at a Funeral
73 / Previous Lives
74 / Gym Day
75 / Thank You For Calling
76 / Handsome Stranger
79 / The Cows Discover Religion
80 / Happy Holidays
81 / Distance
82 / Signs of Intelligent Life
85 / Immigrant
86 / Not All Heroes Wear Capes
87 / Obit
88 / Patience
89 / The Jogger
90 / Compound-Word Adjectives
94 / Invitation
95 / Fabric
96 / Faking It
99 / Status

100 / One Thing
101 / Spooning
102 / Ant Traps
104 / Child of the Decade Award Acceptance Speech, December 31, 1969
107 / Horror Story
109 / The First Day of College Classes, Fall Semester, 2036
112 / Keeping Up
113 / In a Jam
114 / Change is Good?
116 / Double-Shift
117 / My Little Eye
119 / Work Like a Dog
121 / Winter Treat
123 / His First Mistake
124 / Question
125 / New Friends
127 / Sign
128 / Santa Nears Retirement
129 / Dog Attack
131 / What to do When the Neighbors' Dogs Won't Stop Barking for Thirty-Seven Nights in a Row

Keys

When Jamaal arrived at his father's house on Friday evening, he saw the old man standing on the front stoop, facing the door.

Something didn't look quite right as Jamaal approached. His father wore a droopy old jacket, one of the five he had alternated each weekday for the last however many years of teaching math to kids who sometimes paid attention at the local public school, sometimes stared into space as the numbers flew above their heads and out the windows. The jacket seemed to vibrate at a slow pace, almost imperceptible, as his father's right arm, held in a right angle at the elbow, pulsed slightly as if keeping time to snappy jazz no one else could hear.

"Dad?" Jamaal called softly as he approached his father.

The old man turned, his expression a mix of surprise and frustration. "The goddamned door won't unlock," he said, clipping the words like the chalk strokes of another equation on another Friday afternoon.

Jamaal noticed his father held his keys in his right hand, pointing them toward the door and pressing the electric lock for his car door over and over.

"This thing was working this morning!" his father groused, looking at the keys as if they'd said something bad about his dog.

After staring at the keys for a few depressions of the button, Jamaal said in a soft voice, "Dad, that's your car key." He gently maneuvered the key ring in his father's gnarled hand until the house key aligned with the doorknob.

"Well shit," his father said, and then he forced a smile-less chuckle. "I guess I need my head examined!"

Jamaal laughed too as his father easily unlocked the door with the correct key and called over his shoulder, "Are you staying for dinner?"

"Is Mom making meatloaf tonight?" he asked. Even in his fifth decade of life, his mother's meatloaf could make him happy as a carefree child again for the time it took to eat a second helping.

"You know, she might have mentioned something about that this morning," his father replied, sounding his cheerful self again. "But I honestly don't remember."

"I'm only staying if it's meatloaf," Jamaal said, playing along with a joke they'd shared many times.

But Jamaal wondered if his father could sense the concern swimming at snorkel-depth beneath the humor. His father was scheduled to see the neurologist again next week for more tests. Jamaal was going with him this time—at the doctor's request.

Something other than the trip to the doctor was also weighing on Jamaal's mind. Just that morning, he had tried to jam his own house key into his office door's keyhole, briefly pushing and twisting until he scraped his knuckles.

It was only three seconds, a voice in his head assured him. *Doesn't mean a thing.*

Bad Penny

The random coin Fred got in change at the coffee shop was so dirty, worn, and grimy that he had to rub it vigorously with this thumb, hold it right up to his face, and squint to read the date. Yep, that's what he thought—the same year that he was born.

Now is the Winter

As Frank finished clearing the driveway this afternoon, he saw the neighbors' five-year-old son approach.

"When you get too old to shovel," the youngster said, "I'll be old enough to do it for you."

"Bless you, young man," Frank replied between labored breaths. "Please grow quickly."

Loss

All his life, Stan's goal was to "drop a few pounds." He ran a five-minute mile in college, led his recreational league basketball team in scoring each year, and never took a sick day while outworking all the youngsters at the construction site for years.

Stan always thought that if he could just get rid of the small loop of fat around his midsection, then everything in his life would be so much better. He skipped desserts, swore off snacks, and never took the second helpings he craved. Still, the stubborn fat remained for decades.

Then one day, without explanation, he noticed the fat begin to recede.

A year after his diagnosis, as his wife helps lift his skeletal frame from the bed to the wheelchair each morning, Stan longs to have those few pounds back.

Old Trick

Duchess was nineteen—impossibly ancient for a big dog—when Dave brought her to the vet for the last time after a month of lethargy and a week when she didn't eat and rarely left her bed by the fireplace.

For nearly two decades, Duchess had barked at countless delivery trucks, slept in pools of sunshine on hardwood floors for what must add up to entire years, saw three kids off to preschool and eventually to college, ate and pooped a mountain range of kibble, dug enough dirt to bury a city, chased whole universes of squirrels that she never caught.

The vet said, "A good life, a big life." His voice was so kind, like an old, wise friend. "Maybe it's time for her to rest now."

Dave nodded, ignored the stranglehold on his throat, stretched out a hand for one last touch goodbye.

For the first time in weeks, Dave saw Duchess's nose twitch and search, saw a familiar look in her cloudy eyes as she slowly raised her head a last time.

Just seconds from the end of her life, she was checking to see if Dave's hand concealed a treat.

Yesterday's Special

Bang, bang, bang! Nathan's knuckles began to ache in the chill air as he rapped on the window for a fourth time.

Bang, bang, bang! Now a fifth time.

Nathan pressed close to the glass and blocked the morning light by cupping his hands on each side of his face. Finally, he saw Jessika move inside the darkened restaurant, emerging from the tiny, back-room apartment her uncle had set up for her so she could manage the restaurant while earning her degree. Nathan admired her dedication.

Concern lined Jessika's features. She stepped cautiously into the early morning light streaming through the window. When she recognized Nathan as the source of the pounding, her face fell from concern to annoyance. For a moment, Nathan thought her whole face might slide down the front of her oversized flannel shirt all the way to the floor.

Jessika stopped about ten feet from the window and asked, "What the hell do you want?" Nathan couldn't hear her words through the window, but, after nearly six months together, he knew her well enough to read her lips.

"Please let me in," he called out, not loud enough to be sure she heard him through the glass. He didn't want to yell at 6 a.m. on a public street in the middle of town. Even this early, several people were out and about. Joggers jogged. Dog walkers walked their dogs. Fit and trim senior citizens power-strode along the sidewalk, always in pairs, each breath escaping in puffs as white as their hair. These people would live to 100,

Nathan reasoned, all of them, just from moving like this every morning. You can't die if you won't stop moving forward.

"Why?" Jessika's mouth formed the question as her upturned hands implored. Nathan could tell she said it loudly but could only catch a hint of sound.

"Let me in! I can explain!" he shouted back, drawing a few white-haired stares. "Please," he said, softer.

Jessika looked at him, considered, hesitated, and then stepped forward. Nathan side-stepped toward the door, ready for the lock and knob to turn, the bells to rattle, and the metal-framed glass to swing open. Everything would be all right again if he could just talk to her. He'd make coffee. They'd sit at one of the tables near the back. She wasn't scheduled to open for lunch until eleven. He had time. He could make her understand just how sorry he was.

All she had to do was open the door.

Instead, Jessika climbed onto the inside window ledge and sat, yoga style. She pulled a razor blade from her shirt pocket. She didn't even look up at Nathan as he leaned toward the door that wouldn't be opening anytime soon. With the razor, Jessika set to work scraping the leftover color of the former message painted across the inside of the glass.

Nathan watched as the letters "S-P-E-C-I-A-L" disappeared one after another beneath her blade.

Command Decision

General Stratton submitted his retirement papers the morning after he heard the new recruit say he hoped the war would last forever.

Elevator

It wasn't until the third visit to her mother's new "active-senior" apartment building that Karen finally realized what had been bothering her about the elevator. It wasn't the tinny music or the stale scent or the ugly paisley wallpaper.

No, it was the fact that the doors were exactly the width of an ambulance gurney.

Suspect

Josh had been moving all weekend, filling his small truck and hauling load after load from the old apartment to his new house. As a single person in his mid-twenties, for the first time, he felt like such a grown-up, such a "real person," for having gone through all of the house-buying tasks that seemed so endless when he first walked into the bank four months ago. They gave him about a thousand pages of forms to fill out and, after countless meetings, phone calls, and credit explanation letters, he had finally been approved and closed on the mortgage for the little cape on the country lane just last week. Josh was now a homeowner—but one last step remained. He actually had to move into his new home.

Compared with a family of four, Josh didn't have much stuff, but it seemed like a lot because he was moving it all himself during a single weekend to save money. He packed all week and began moving Saturday morning at six, before the summer heat got intense, ate on the run when he could, and collapsed into bed that night at nine. He was up and working again at six Sunday morning, retracing the ten-mile route between the apartment and house again and again. He looked forward to sleeping in his new house for the first time that night. In fact, his bed was the last item packed onto the truck for the last trip as the late afternoon slipped into early evening. On the way, he decided to stop at McDonald's and get a burger so that he didn't pass out from hunger.

This McDonald's had one of those playscapes that kids love. As Josh stood in line waiting to order, he watched a group of children rollicking in a huge bin of plastic balls, diving out of site and emerging to scream with delight. They couldn't possibly ever have more fun in their lives than they were having right at that moment.

One mother had just finished corralling her two kids and herded them toward the exit. As they passed him, Josh couldn't help but stare. They were completely delightful: a boy and a girl, maybe a year or so apart, just a shade under three feet tall, each clad in jeans with the cuffs folded up over their tiny scale models of adult-style basketball shoes, ketchup stains on their faces and shirts. As a new homeowner, Josh thought about meeting a nice woman who would want to have kids just like these to fill their hearts and the second bedroom in the new house. He liked that thought.

Josh smiled at the kids and said hi as they paused on their way toward the exit to gaze up at him with their big, curious kids' eyes.

Their mother quickly pulled them toward the door, hissing, "Let's go ... *we don't know him.*"

Josh glanced up to see her give him a look so dirty it would wither a perennial. She glared at him her whole way to the door, then hustled the kids into a minivan and sped away. Josh had no idea what he had done to deserve such a look.

He got his burger and unwrapped it on the way to the truck, inhaling the addictive fat odor and taking the first bite. When he reached for his door handle, he got a look at his reflection in the driver-side window. Josh had to admit that he wasn't a pretty sight.

Sweat stained his armpits and actually seeped out to meet in the middle of his chest, forming a Mickey Mouse silhouette. His unwashed hair was plastered to his head. Cobwebs dangled from his beard. Scratches and bruises lined his forearms from carrying boxes, furniture, and other assorted possessions that he couldn't bring himself to toss out. His jeans were shiny from wiping sweaty palms on them.

And his zipper was down.

It wasn't just down. It was way down, down all the way and gaping open to reveal his underwear—underwear that was, Josh was ashamed to admit, sweat-stained and filthy.

Needless to say, he was horrified to be out in public looking like this. But at least he now knew why the woman had yanked her kids away from him. She must have figured he was some kind of pervert on the prowl for his next victim. Josh quickly pulled up his zipper as he ducked into the privacy of his driver's seat, covered his wild hair with a hat, raked the webs from his beard, and promised himself a hot shower when he got to the new house.

As he approached the parking lot exit, a police cruiser pulled in with its lights flashing. It dawned on Josh that the woman must have called 9-1-1 from her cell phone as she was leaving McDonald's, hoping to protect other mothers' children from the wild man on the loose. The officers gave Josh sharp-eyed looks as they passed, so he nodded to them, and then dutifully engaged his turn signal, doing his best to look like the respectable, property-owning citizen he knew himself to be as he drove toward his new home and his new life.

How Much?

Minutes before the job interview, Taylor somehow let more than a foot of her skirt dip into the toilet she had just nervously used down the hall from her potential new employer.

"Oh, shit," she said, struck by the uncommonly literal meaning of that common swear.

"How much do I need this job?' she asked herself aloud, noticing the clarity of echo emanating in the contained space. She also noticed the clarity of her answer.

"A lot," Taylor said as she grabbed a wad of paper towels, got a handful of antibacterial soap from the dispenser, and set to work.

How One Thing Leads to Another

The day had warmed from the chilly morning to the temperate afternoon, so he paid his lunch check, left his coat on the back of his chair, and stepped into the sunshine of the parking lot.

If he had remembered to put on his coat, he wouldn't have noticed a fragment of lint on the front of his shirt. If he hadn't noticed the lint, he would have seen the low air pressure in his front driver-side tire. If he had noticed the low air pressure, he would also have noticed the sluggish handling of his car as he negotiated the entrance ramp to the highway on the way home. If he had noticed the sluggish handling, he would have been more prepared to deal with the downed branch that blocked part of the entrance ramp merging onto the interstate. If he had been more prepared to deal with the branch, he might not have overcorrected his steering and let his passenger-side front tire slip off the pavement onto the gravel. If he hadn't let his passenger-side front tire slip onto the gravel, he wouldn't have flipped his car over the embankment where it rolled seven times before coming to rest in the backyard of a cute little ranch-style house. If he hadn't flipped into this particular backyard, his future wife wouldn't have run out of the cute little ranch-style house to make sure he was okay.

If he hadn't met his future wife, who would have gotten him a new coat for Christmas that year?

Motive

"Every morning when they were on vacation, their alarm went off at 5 a.m.," Frank said, looking down at the young cop's shiny shoes. "*Every. Single. Morning.* For two weeks. I couldn't take it anymore, officer."

Scotty had been on the job just three months, mostly directing traffic at the middle school, helping senior citizens carry groceries, and trying not to look as scared as he felt. He still wasn't used to being called "officer." This was the first time he had to use his handcuffs.

The houses in this neighborhood, Scotty noticed, were packed along the street with barely ten feet separating them. Windows had views into other windows.

"Sorry, sir," Scotty said, gently guiding Frank into the back seat of his patrol car, palming his balding head to keep him from bumping it on the door frame. "I can sympathize, but breaking-and-entering is still a crime."

Too Wild

Randy washed his hands with his back to the restroom door. In the mirror, he saw someone enter and walk to the row of urinals on the opposite wall. All he could make out were bulky clothes and a thick head of dark hair.

Randy dried his hands and turned to leave, not looking at the new arrival. Just as he grasped the door handle, the man at the urinal called out without looking, "Hey, guy? You leaving?"

Randy stopped. He could have kept going, but there was something in the man's voice that said he was both harmless and risky at the same time.

"I was," Randy replied.

"Come over here first," the man said.

Randy hesitated.

"C'mon," the man beckoned, looking at Randy for the first time. Salt-and-pepper stubble covered a rugged face, not handsome but also not not-handsome. His midsection was thrust into the urinal. His hands held something there, just out of Randy's view. Whatever it was, it seemed to be moving.

Randy let his fingers slip from the door handle.

"I've got something that I think you'll want to see," the man said, smiling. "Nothing to be shy about."

Randy took small, tentative steps toward the man.

"What is it?" Randy asked, his question quivering in the restroom echo-chamber.

"You'll like it," the man said, sales pitch in his voice.

"I've never done anything like this before," Randy said.

The man nodded with empathy. "First time for everything, my friend," he said. "Come closer. You'll want to get a good look." He leaned back slightly.

Randy inched forward until he could see what the man held within the urinal's shadowy porcelain cave.

At first, Randy couldn't make sense of what he saw in the man's hands. It looked to be less than a foot long, rust-colored, and furry. The man held it cautiously, almost tenderly.

Randy thought for a second that it might be a bunny. Then the ears flattened as it hissed, and Randy realized it was a hunched-up, full-grown cat, probably a bit feral, maybe a street cat. Despite its aggressive bearing, something about it was peculiarly inviting, so Randy reached out to it.

"Go ahead," the man said, turning now to reveal the fur bundle swaddled in the bottom of his bulky jacket. When the cat saw Randy's hands coming closer, its hiss turned to a soft meow. "I think he likes you," the man said.

The man released the cat, and Randy gathered it into his hands and lifted it to his chest. The cat instantly started purring and rubbing its face against Randy's chin.

"That's so beautiful," the man said, seeming to hold back tears. "He's yours now."

The man turned quickly and strode toward the door. It was Randy's turn to call out to him. "Hey, wait a second. What's his name?"

The man gave Randy a last smile. "He was too wild for me, so I couldn't name him. You tamed him. You get to name him."

Then he was gone, and the cat's life was changed forever. Randy's life, too, would never be the same.

Curt Had a Great Deal of Anger

For the third time this month, Curt got called into the boss's office and reamed out because his job performance was in the toilet. *Who gives a crap about the way I answer my phone?* Curt thought as he stomped back to his cubicle.

Last week the complaint had been about the sloppy way he filled out a complicated but essential form that he wrongly assumed no one ever read. *Those forms could be put to better use wiping my ass.* The week before, it had been for spending too much time away from his desk. *I get my work done, so I'm not gonna sit around this dump any more than I have to.*

Curt decided to get even with his boss. *I know what I'll do,* he thought as his face flushed and he shoved open the door to the office restroom, the one on the north hallway that the boss used most often. *I'll eat nothing but high-fiber cereal every morning and take a big crap in here every day, twice a day if I can, even three times, and I won't flush, never. Just let it all sit there for that big jerk to find. That'll show him. He can't mess with me.*

Curt sat in his cubicle, stared at his boss's office door, and caressed his MAGA hat in its secret hiding place beneath his desk.

Yes, Curt certainly had a great deal of anger. But, unfortunately, Curt didn't have much of anything else.

When?

Christopher wondered when he became the guy who needed two energy drinks each morning, nodded off during afternoon meetings, and then took three different pills to fall asleep each night.

TMI

Russell wasn't happy about the new toilets at work. Gone were the standard models that flushed when he lifted his foot and stepped on the handle. Russell had always enjoyed the athletic accomplishment of being middle-aged but able to balance while he stood on his left foot and depressed the handle with his right. *Still got it,* he thought each time. Sometimes he even did a little fist-pump when his bad shoulder wasn't acting up.

But the new toilets, installed six months ago, flushed automatically. Russell didn't know how they worked, but when he stood after doing his business, the toilets flushed on their own. Maybe it was an electric eye or a weight sensor on the seat. All three of the toilets in the restroom closest to his office worked that way. Even the ones in the restroom one floor down and one floor up worked that way. He didn't try the ones on the floors higher and lower than that. *Might as well go home if I have to go that far,* he reasoned.

Russell realized the other day that he's probably spent more time in this work restroom during the past two decades than he has in his bathrooms at home. The downstairs one has the best wifi connection for playing Words with Friends, and the upstairs one has the best magazines. Those rooms are fine, but they're both "bath" rooms. His family members bathe there. This is a "rest" room. He comes here for solace, solitude, reflection, and just to get away from Wilkinstan, the jerk in the next office who watches Fox News clips at full volume and reads aloud from Breitbart articles all day long.

The problem with the new self-flushing toilets was that they flushed so quickly, Russell was never finished using the toilet paper. He didn't think that he took an inordinate amount of time using the toilet paper. But, each time, the toilet flushed long before he was ready to drop the first wad of paper into the bowl, let alone the second and, sometimes, third. The toilets no longer had a manual flush option, and Russell thought it would be rude to leave wads of used toilet paper there to greet the next occupant.

Always up for a challenge, Russell began working to outsmart these new toilets. For months, he experimented to understand the exact timing and circumstances of the automatic flush. They all took the same exact three seconds to flush after he stood. He admired the consistency if not the rapidity.

Russell was nothing if not a problem solver. Eventually, he discovered that he could rise slowly, hover just above the seat, and delay the automatic flush. If he went up six inches, he could hang out there as long as his thigh muscles could hold him, and there would be no flush. At seven inches, he had the same three seconds he had when he stood all the way. Six inches was the magic distance.

So he started wiping as he hovered at low altitude, delaying the flush. But that made it hard to get the two or three wads of toilet paper he needed before his legs began to ache. So he learned to prepare the paper while still seated, placing wads somewhere in his lap for easy access, sometimes tucking them into a crotch crevice to keep them from rolling off onto the floor.

Eventually, six months after the automatic-flushers' installation, Russell perfected his technique. He could make it work each time without prematurely engaging the automatic flush. The hover maneuver, (as he'd come to call it) required strong thigh muscles and engaging his core for balance, so it replaced the athletic satisfaction he felt with his former one-foot flush. Now, instead of the frustration he felt at the too-quick automatic flush, he felt pride in his painstakingly developed technique for beating the system. The toilet paper went down with everything else in one flush, and all was as it should be in that private moment.

Who can I tell about all this? Russell wondered, walking back to his office. Who would want to hear this story and share his accomplishment? He couldn't think of anyone, not even his closest friends and family members. Definitely not his coworkers, who must have their own personalized ceremonies for dealing with the renovated restrooms. He sure as hell wasn't telling that jerk Wilkinstan.

Maybe he could tell strangers. Russell wouldn't stop them on the street and say, "Hey, listen, we got these new toilets at work, you see, and ..." The rest of the story would get him strange looks at best. More likely, arrested. Or punched.

Maybe he could write the story down, first by hand in the little notebook on his bedside table that his wife got him last year for recording interesting thoughts. The notebook was still empty, so there would be plenty of pages. Then he could type the story on his computer, spend some time with it, revise, tinker, edit, get every word just right.

Then Russell could email it to a special stranger who might copy and paste it and code it for display on the internet, perhaps in an online literary journal. Maybe other strangers would come to read it, to share the experiences of even more strangers who put their thoughts in writing. Maybe this story, humble as it was, could inspire people out there in the wide world in some way that went beyond a simple story about toilets. Maybe this story meant something more than its literal telling. Maybe this was really a story about humanity rising above and reaching beyond. What was that fancy literary word that Russell learned in college? Oh, yes: *allegory*. Maybe this was Russell's own personal allegory that the world should read.

Nah. Never gonna happen, Russell decided as he walked back to his desk. *Better just to keep it to myself.*

Breakdown Lane

Even after fifteen minutes pulled off of the interstate, steam still flowed from the hood of Jessica's car. *Oh well,* she thought as she leaned against the back bumper, prepared to wait for the tow truck that she knew wouldn't be here for at least an hour. *Look on the bright side?* she thought, more of a question than a directive to herself. She finally had the perfect opportunity to contemplate her life's many dead ends, wrong turns, and broken-down moments.

Third Date

The realization hit him halfway through dinner (when she wiped his milk mustache and told him how much he reminded her of her little brother) that the evening would end with a handshake.

Christmas Eve

Howie's parents sat on the living room love seat, exchanging family gifts, their family's long-time Christmas Eve tradition. Dad opened his present first: an anti-fog shower mirror. Mom went next: a collection of chemical-free bath soaps.

"Thank you so much, Bill," his mom said, kissing his dad on the cheek in the glow of the Christmas tree.

"You're so welcome, Annie," his dad replied, squeezing her hand.

They're so cute, Howie thought. *But so old.* He knew that they hiked each weekend and took a yoga class together. "Active seniors" was the term Howie had heard to describe them—although they were just beyond fifty. Howie had recently turned twenty-one while a junior in college. From his perspective, fifty wasn't much different from one hundred fifty.

Howie thanked his parents for the package of socks and underwear. He actually wore the annual gifts every day of the upcoming year and would be shocked and slightly disappointed if they ever got him a new phone or a car.

"Are you going out tonight," Howie's dad asked him.

"Of course!" Howie replied.

"What time," his mom inquired.

"Soon," Howie said, glancing at his phone.

"That's great," his dad said. "Have fun!"

"When are you getting yourself a girlfriend?" Howie's mom asked him.

Howie laughed. "Never!" he said, thinking about the dozen girls back at college he could call for "no-strings" get-togethers. He wasn't interested in accelerating the process of becoming just another cute, boring, old married couple.

Little did Howie know what had happened between Bill and Annie on that love seat the night before, beautifully illuminated by those Christmas lights encircling the tree. Or how his parents would position that shower mirror at just the right angle to reveal the ways that they would put those bath soaps to good use while Howie partied with his buddies later that night. Hiking was great for endurance, yoga for flexibility.

"Merry Christmas!" Howie called out to his parents as he left for Christmas Eve reverie with his happy young friends. *Yes, it is,* Bill and Annie both thought as they held hands and leaned toward each other on the loveseat.

May I Take Your Order?

Monday afternoon, with only twenty minutes to get to another meeting downtown, Aaron waited in line for a drive-thru cheeseburger. As the family in the van in front of him ordered enough food to feed a small country, he realized this would be the only peaceful moment he'd have all week.

How We All Found Out

Marlee couldn't sleep, what with all that worry over her mother moving into the senior home down in Florida. So she sat on her Maine back porch, sipping hot cider in the wee October hours, watching falling stars while Nate slept. She stopped thinking about her mother when she realized that way more stars were falling tonight than other worried nights. And then she noticed many of those falling stars changing direction, hovering over the woods, and slowly descending. Then Marlee yelled for Nate and grabbed her fancy new camera phone.

The next day, of course, we all found out.

Finish Line

While running his first marathon at age fifty, Jake finally spotted the finish line ahead. But why was that finish line bathed in a tunnel of heavenly light? And was that Jake's grandmother floating there, waving and calling him to her?

Frosty Walk

Longing to know the difference it would make, Robert took the road less traveled and stubbed his toe after three steps. He took the road less traveled and stepped in a dog turd with his new hiking boots. He took the road less traveled and found an abundance of biting flies, toadstools, and browning ferns. He took the road less traveled and had to run to escape a foam-mouthed, snarling dog. He took the road less traveled and found the back half of a rusting VW microbus. He took the road less traveled and smelled something rotten, likely a dead animal. He took the road less traveled and emerged behind a fast-food dumpster swarmed by wasps. He took the road less traveled and longed for the Advil in his medicine cabinet. Robert took the road less traveled and scheduled arthroscopic surgery three weeks later, and that has made all the difference.

Tough Enough

During his week-long trip from Kansas to Colorado with his wife and teenaged son, Oscar let his beard grow in. That's why he looked so facially awkward on the trip. There's probably a support group somewhere for this condition: not-quite-a-beard syndrome. But you can only be in the support group for a few weeks before they give you a pat on the back and tell you that you're cured, and you have to go away because there are people out there with real problems.

Oscar thought the whole beard thing would give him that tough, outdoorsy, Western look for his trip. But Oscar wasn't in Kansas anymore. Looking tough was a little difficult on this particular trip because of his pronounced fear of heights. So when the family hiked up six-inch-wide switchback trails on an exposed Rocky Mountain ridge at ten thousand feet, his son skipped along, head down and checking for cell phone service, and his wife floated like a ballerina across gaps in the trail over head-spinning drop-offs. But Oscar had to hug his hiking poles click-clacking on the rocks while he sobbed quietly, unnoticed by his nearby family—well, he just didn't look much like the Marlboro Man.

Oscar's fear of heights was most entertaining when the family visited the famous ancient Pueblo cliff dwellings carved into canyons a thousand feet above the river. His beard didn't help much when he cowered against the back wall while grandparent tourists teetered happily half a step from certain death as their eight-year-old grandson yanked on his arm, dragging him toward the edge, shouting in his face, "Hey, mister, c'mon! Check out this killer view!"

It was damned hard to look tough with that happening. That's why Oscar shaved as soon as he got back home to Kansas. Life was tough enough in the flatlands for an actuarial at Yellow Brick Insurance who knew the mortality rate for tourists at high altitude. As Dorothy, who overcame her own height-related issues, would say, *there's no place like home.*

Middle-Aged Man's First Text Message

Hi Sweetie. I'm in the bathroom at work. I forgot to bring a book to read. But I have my phone, so I'm texting. See you tonight. Love, John.

New

See how relaxed the shiny new snow blower is as it soaks up the afternoon sunshine in the peaceful corner of the parking lot. See how content, how innocent, how happy it is in its radiant blue factory-issue paint job, a blue bluer even than today's sky. See how it responds to the touch of strong, leather-gloved hands guiding it to its home just inside the garage-bay door. Does it suspect that a white monster will approach in the night, stalking in darkness until tomorrow's daybreak blitzkrieg blizzard attack? Does it wonder who is predator? Who is prey? Who can say?

The Cover-Story-Warm-Up Reader Guy

No matter how much he wanted to, Scott couldn't write stories of his own. So he decided to become a cover-story-warm-up reader guy. Singers who didn't write their own songs performed hits by famous bands, so why couldn't he "cover" famous writers?

Scott showed up at local libraries, bookstores, colleges, coffeeshops—anywhere writers were reading stories. Before the "real" author took the stage, Scott would read a few stories from anthologies of classic authors: John Updike, Sidonie-Gabrielle Colette, Shirley Jackson, Nathaniel Hawthorne, Kate Chopin, Edgar Allen Poe, Ernest Hemingway, Raymond Carver, William Faulkner, Herman Melville.

For a while, Scott was content with his role. Much as concert-goers could tolerate and even sometimes appreciate a warm-up cover band, fans of live literature managed to sit through his cover-story-warm-up readings. He didn't get paid in a monetary sense, but the polite applause and cheese-and-cracker tables sustained him, much as the mild approval and mediocre meals provided by his parents got him through those long years of childhood.

But then an audience member asked Scott how he felt about reading such depressing stories by long-dead authors. He couldn't answer. And some of the actual authors featured at the local readings asked him if he wrote his own stories. They were just making polite conversation during the awkward moments following these readings when audience members milled about, not wanting to stay but having no other plans for the night, literature being their only hobby.

Scott knew he couldn't write his own stories, but, as a human being, he needed a creative outlet, so he started changing the gloomy endings to the classics he read. Sammy toughed it out and kept his job at the A&P, eventually getting promoted to store manager. The young bride learned to communicate how she wanted her husband to touch her with his monstrous hand. The lottery-winner got an extra helping of pie at the town picnic, where not a single stone flew. Wakefield stayed home where he belonged. Mrs. Mallard embraced her rescued husband, joy healing her damaged heart. Montresor and Fortunato enjoyed a few too many glasses of wine and then drifted off to pleasant slumber. Francis Macomber shot straight and lived long. The splitting couple sought mediation, and their issue was decided amicably with no harm to the innocent baby. Emily married happily, snuggled with a warm body, and paid her local taxes.

Audiences barely noticed Scott's revisions. Even among the type of people who frequented literary readings, surprisingly few had read the classics. But, eventually, a few English majors objected, claiming that great literature couldn't be molded by the whims of just anyone. The tipping point came when Scott tried to marry Bartleby to the boss's daughter and award him an employee-of-the-month certificate. After that, he was insistently requested to forego his role as the cover-story-warm-up reader guy.

As for the ending of his own story, these days, Scott maintains an Instagram account under the handle, "F. Scott." To put food on his table, he drives a bland delivery truck and wears a brown uniform. He prefers the boxes large and heavy. The slim ones might contain a book, and Scott has given up on those.

Upping her Game

After Janet skidded about thirty car lengths on the icy interstate, she realized that she had quite a bit of work to do if she ever hoped to be quoted in a book of meaningful last words by famous people.

The First Five Pages

When Edgar was twenty-three and imagining himself to be a writer, he met Kurt Vonnegut. Vonnegut was an author so famous that he really had no business giving a lecture at the second-rate graduate school where Edgar skipped classes in Colonial American Poetry and Deconstructionist Literary Theory to read 1950s science fiction novels and scratch out short stories for hours at a time in the window booth of the pizza place on Main Street.

The day after Vonnegut's lecture, as Edgar sat in that pizza place, the great author himself walked in with the English department chair trailing along behind and talking nonstop long after Vonnegut had ceased listening politely.

Edgar knew a pivotal moment when he saw one. He walked right by that befuddled department chair and pushed a heap of paper toward Vonnegut, the only famous writer Edgar had ever seen in the flesh.

"Would you read my story, Mr. Vonnegut?" Edgar asked, looking directly into the great man's face. Vonnegut took the story without hesitation, methodically counted out the first five pages like a cash register kid counting change on his first day of work, gripped them tightly, ripped them away from the staple with one clean pull, and handed them back to Edgar.

With a look of grandfatherly patience, Vonnegut said, "You keep these. At your age, the first five pages just say, 'Hey, look at me. I'm a nice person writing a story. Please like me and like my story.' Nobody needs that crap."

Vonnegut patted Edgar's staring face, those first five pages drooping in the younger man's sweaty hand.

The department chair gave Edgar a dirty look that he pretended not to notice. Vonnegut folded the rest of Edgar's story and stuck it in his back pocket as he walked away. "If I like this, I'll find out who you are," he said with a wave, "and you'll hear from me."

That was thirty years ago. Edgar never heard a word.

Mystery Story

One guy was dead. The other guy held a gun, which was literally smoking when the police broke down the locked door. The guy with the gun was mumbling something about a woman they both loved. It really didn't seem like much of a mystery.

But, hey, you never know.

Somewhere Down There

Somewhere down there in his memory, his high school long since torn down and hauled away to fill a landfill, buried beneath the rubble of countless other demolitions among the gray hard jagged chunks of locker room concrete blocks, among the crushed red brick walls whose sight he cursed each morning from the school bus, among the shattered hallway tiles he shuffled over on yet another trip to the principal's office, within the mangled gym lockers used by his basketball team so bad their own fans booed them, inside his very own senior year locker is his pair of "lucky" socks worn the last game of the year, another loss, somewhere down there, through the rubble, through the decades, through the memories—those lucky socks still stink.

What to do After College

Fill your head with dirt: rich, dark topsoil. Plant flowers in your ears: daisies or azaleas. Grow trees in your eye-sockets: butternut or cottonwood. Cultivate food crops in your nose: corn, potatoes, grains. Plow them with your tongue. Mulch with corpuscles. Irrigate with saliva.

Your brain? Keep it for amusement. Donate it to science. Or chop it up for fertilizer.

Reflection

While she went off to find a new set of bed sheets, he lingered in the bath section. He studied himself in the first mirror, but it was only 3X power. All he saw was the need for a shave. The second was stronger, 5X, but that only revealed a few freckles he didn't know were there. The last mirror was the most powerful. But even in its 10X reflection, he was satisfied that she wouldn't see what he was searching for in his face: guilt for what had caused them to need new bed sheets in the first place.

Room 211

"Are you sick?" Sarah's boss, Julia, said, poking her head in Sarah's office door. "Your face is so red."

"No! I'm fine!" Sarah protested. She wondered if the strange tone to her voice was as obvious to everyone else as it was to her. "I just got back from lunch. It's windy out there."

"Okay, carry on," Julia said, ducking out as quickly as she had arrived. "You just look a little flushed," she called as she retreated down the hallway. "Maybe a little under the weather," her words drifting away with the click of her heels.

Sarah didn't have her usual brown bag lunch in the park across the street today. Instead, she skipped lunch and drove to the motel a few miles away on the outskirts of town. She had spent today's lunch hour in room 211 with a man she'd met at a party a few weeks ago. The party was at Julia's house. The man's name was Robb. Robb was Julia's husband.

After a moment lost in pleasurable thoughts of today's lunch hour, Sarah heard her computer ping with the arrival of a new email message. It was Julia: *No problem if you need to go home. You work so hard and never take sick days. We can reschedule the meeting and get by without you for the afternoon.*

Sarah's phone vibrated. Robb texted: *Let's do that again soon. Very soon.*

Sarah replied to Julia's email: *Maybe you're right. Just this once. See you tomorrow. Thanks.*

A few minutes later, Sarah was in the parking lot, striding into the stiff wind on her way to her car, tapping a text message to Robb into her phone. *How soon?*

How about now? Room 211 was paid for until tomorrow morning, but she and Robb wouldn't need that much time.

No

Yes, the orthopedic surgeon looks kind of young, Gary thought as he lay on the operating table, settling in for the procedure that would repair his torn anterior cruciate ligament and eventually allow him to rejoin his friends for their Tuesday-evening "old guy" basketball games at the health club.

Yes, I'm old enough to be his father, Gary thought, but the kid did graduate from medical school, and he must have observed dozens of ACL reconstructions, and then assisted in dozens more with experienced surgeons.

The nurse had laughed when she gave him the pen and asked him to write "NO" in big letters on his left knee, the one that had always been strong and healthy, had always managed to compensate for the weak and balky right one, to make sure that the surgeon operated on the right knee, the correct one.

I'll be okay, Gary thought, just as the anesthesiologist said, "Count backward from 100," and Gary barely made it to 97, 96, 9- ... before the ceiling lights began to swirl and darkness closed around him.

When Gary awoke in the recovery room, he was surprised to see several doctors, nurses, and people in business suits so formal that they could be arguing before the Supreme Court gathered around his bed, each with a concerned expression, so he asked, just before the pain pounded into his knee through the fading effects of the anesthesia, "What happened?"

"From certain angles," the young orthopedic surgeon said, stepping out from the hiding place behind his elders and barely managing to look Gary in the eye, "the word 'NO' looks a lot like the word 'ON.'"

Post-Op

It was only minor surgery, after all—snip a little cartilage and drain some fluid. An hour after it was over, hearing his name called, Dennis slipped in and out of awareness. His throat burned from the breathing tube they'd removed. He longed for ice chips fed by his loving wife, the laughter of his children, a nuzzle from the family dog. The pain throbbed but was less than what he'd been told to expect. The bed sheets scratched his face, and he felt heavy against the mattress. As the hours passed, he grew gradually lighter, more aware, and finally lifted himself from the bed. By evening, he wanted to go home.

A week later, after his funeral, Dennis felt fully himself again, ready to haunt those he had left behind, starting with the doctors and nurses who had let him die.

Does this Hurt?

"Does this hurt?" she asked.

The physical therapist had one hand on the back of Bill's thigh and the other grasped around his ankle. She pushed the ankle toward his butt, encountering resistance even though she wasn't even close to a ninety-degree angle.

Bill's face pressed into the naughahyde-covered table. His glasses jutted halfway off his face, smashed into the bridge of his nose, and poked into his left eyeball. The naughahyde smelled exactly like the cheap, inflatable wading pool he had splashed around in as a kid.

"Does this hurt?" she asked again, a little louder this time, while forcing his knee an excruciating inch farther.

Bill's lips had become vacuum-sealed to the naughahyde, so he rolled his head a bit to the right to free up his mouth in an attempt to answer her. There was a little suction "pop" when his mouth disengaged from the table. But even with his mouth now open, the only sound that escaped was a faint gasp.

She pushed his leg another inch. He could actually hear unidentified fleshy material inside his knee tearing.

"Bill?" she asked once more, very loud and clear this time. *"Does this hurt?"*

He really wanted to answer. The physical therapist was an intelligent, nice person who went out of her way to be pleasant company during these difficult sessions. Bill wanted to summon a calm voice to pronounce the word "yes" with clarity and dignity. He didn't want to remain silent and unresponsive, but his wide-open mouth just wouldn't form a coherent word.

When Bill finally managed to get sound to make its way up from his throat and out into the world, he screamed like a five-year-old whose mean older brother had just ripped the legs off his favorite G.I. Joe.

What Kills Us

Ellis woke at an hour when military clocks employ a zero. He stumbled to the dark bathroom and emptied his bladder, always a relief for a man of middle age. When he blew his nose, he noticed by the moonlight leaking through the window a small spot of blood on the tissue.

What could a wee-hours micro-nosebleed mean? Harbinger of some disease so horrible it could only be spoken of by its initials? An early turn toward a slow, painful decline? Or the only hint of a random dark-of-night seizure stalking his brain to attack on a calendar square yet to be turned?

Or did Ellis simply sleep that night with his neck bent to press his nose too long into a pointy pillow corner? Omens aren't always omens. Sometimes they're just awkward sleeping positions and the age-induced minor weakening of vulnerable nasal membranes.

If life had taught Ellis anything, it had taught him that, in the end, what kills us seldom warns us.

Six Dreams that Might Not Be Dreams

(1) As a child, he often dreamed of being chased by a mummy. He was running as fast as he could through the woods while the mummy was staggering slowly, tripping over roots and stones, bumping into trees, holding its arms in front of itself like a bad movie cliché. Even so, the damned thing was still catching up to him.

(2) As an adolescent, he sometimes dreamed about falling from a high cliff near the rural church his family attended. In the real world, the cliff was only about four feet high, and the kids jumped off of it on a dare after an hour of listening to the minister negotiate for their eternal souls. In his dream, the cliff was hundreds of feet high, thousands, maybe bottomless. He didn't scream as he fell, but instead squeezed his eyes shut on the way down, feeling himself accelerate and expecting to hit the ground and die. Instead, he awoke with his eyes shut so tight that his whole face hurt.

(3) His last year of high school, he dreamed of playing softball at recess between classes. It was weird to think that they actually still had recess in twelfth grade, but his school was different that way. On the last day of the school year, he hit a home run that went so far the outfielders searched for hours but couldn't find the ball.

(4) He once dreamed of getting five root canals at the same time, all on his upper right side. The dentist kept asking how often he brushed, why he took so long between dentist visits, what he thought his teeth would look like when he reached middle age. Did he even

want to have his own teeth when he was an old man? the dentist demanded to know.

(5) Even after years of teaching hundreds of classes, he dreamed that he was sitting at the desk in front of a classroom full of students who weren't paying attention to him and even actively ignoring him. He was about to try to get their attention and get the lesson back on track when he realized that he was naked from the waist down, temporarily hidden behind the big, wooden desk.

(6) He dreamed he was halfway up Mount Washington when something popped in his foot as he stepped from one rock to another on the rugged trail. This was the first time he had tried to climb this mountain, and it was also going to be the last time because he was getting too old for shit like this. He wasn't sure if he should limp back down the bottom half of the mountain or limp the uphill half to the top. The only thing he knew for sure was that his foot really hurt, and he would never do this again.

Flaws

During their latest argument, Denise counted off Walt's worst flaws—all eight of them—lifting a finger or thumb for each one. She probably could have named ten flaws, but she was using two fingers to hold her cigarette.

Cheat

As Caroline cheated at solitaire, pulling the ace of hearts from her hiding place within the deck, she asked her husband Ron, immersed in the World Series of Poker on television, "Do you ever think about other women?"

Services

No one in the congregation knew much about their new minister, young Reverend Ashcroft. He just showed up one Sunday morning and told everyone that Reverend Dunbar (who was eighty years old) had retired. Attendance at the church had been dwindling for years, well before Reverend Ashcroft's arrival. And, frankly, few people were paying attention as he muddled through his first sermon. But when he lifted his arms above his head in prayer, everyone saw the jagged, purple scars on the inner sides of each wrist. Reverend Ashcroft was pleasantly surprised when more worshippers occupied the pews the following Sunday.

Mr. Boots

The last thing Bruce wanted to do while driving through upstate New York was stop at the highway rest area—but he had to. So he brought in a book, locked the stall door, and sat down.

After a moment, someone came in and sat in the next stall. The new neighbor was wearing huge work boots that must have been about size sixteen, so Bruce named him, "Mr. Boots." After a moment, Mr. Boots began whispering very softly. Bruce couldn't tell if he were whispering to him or to himself or to someone else. Bruce couldn't make out any of the words. He wasn't even sure they actually were words.

Then Bruce heard a strange crinkling sound, followed by repeated crunching and more crinkling. He was confused for about half a minute, but then it hit him: Mr. Boots was eating chips while sitting on a public toilet.

Without warning, a chip fell to the floor and skittered a couple of inches into Bruce's stall. It was one of those curlicue corn chips that Bruce really liked, so salty and satisfying.

Both men sat in silence for a long ten seconds.

Finally, Mr. Boots asked in a clear, intelligent, almost refined voice, "Are you going to eat that?"

"No, thank you," Bruce replied.

"Okay," Mr. Boots said, and he reached down to pluck the chip from the floor with a large, clean, well-manicured hand. The hand and the chip disappeared from Bruce's view, moving upward.

A fraction of a second later, Bruce heard the crunch.

Sunday Night

Anne's ex-husband Michael dropped off the kids late and unfed, again, tracked mud all the way to the upstairs bathroom, and, as usual, neglected to flush the toilet. Later that night, Michael texted Anne: "Maybe we could give this one more try, baby?"

Seeing Red

Anthony hated reckless drivers, but he hated being late even more. And that was why he blew through the traffic light a full second after it clicked from yellow to red. He hated the way everyone looked at him as he walked in after the meeting had started, judging him, and the power of that shame drove his foot down onto the accelerator instead of the brake. Then, just a few hundred yards beyond the intersection, Anthony was reminded of something he hated even more than reckless drivers and arriving late at meetings: police lights flashing in his rearview mirror.

Thirty-Nine Random, Inappropriate Thoughts at a Funeral

1) It was just a couple of times back in college, kind of experimental. It doesn't make me gay.
2) Wow, look at her! She's my third cousin, I think. That's distant enough.
3) I can't be the only person who thinks the *Harry Potter* movies were better than the *Lord of the Rings* series.
4) It's been a month. How long does it take for the god-damned Prozac to kick in?
5) My butt hurts.
6) If I keep putting the underwear that I've just washed into the top of my underwear drawer, then those will be the first ones I grab to wear, and they will wear out a lot faster than the ones at the bottom of the drawer. I need to start a rotating system before any real damage is done.
7) They couldn't have spent very much on that ugly coffin.
8) I'd have to live to be 300 to pay back all of my student loans.
9) He slept with her and her and her and her and probably her and maybe her.
10) I just went half an hour ago. I can't believe I have to go again.
11) Mental note: Erase the cache of porn links on the work computer.
12) This minister looks like one of those evil priests from a Stephen King movie.

13) Just sit right back and you'll hear a tale, a tale of a fateful trip, that started from this tropic port, aboard this tiny ship.
14) I know we were married for ten years, but I just didn't feel like saying hi to her today. Is that such a crime?
15) Was that a fart or someone's chair squeaking?
16) Man, that guy must have put on eighty pounds since high school.
17) If the Sox's starters don't give them seven good innings every game, they're screwed with the crappy bullpen they've got this year.
18) I can't believe she's wearing white shoes in October. And I can't believe I noticed.
19) I have no idea how much she paid for those breasts, but she sure got her money's worth.
20) The Loch Ness Monster? Maybe. But Bigfoot? That's just ridiculous.
21) If I cough while I yawn, maybe no one will notice that I'm yawning.
22) Sure, they're not the biggest bunch up there, but my flowers are pretty damned impressive.
23) I hope they have those little sandwiches with the crust cut off.
24) Of course it makes a noise. How could a whole big tree fall in a forest and not make any noise?
25) What the hell is a throttle body assembly? I think that mechanic is trying to rip me off again.
26) If Ferguson thinks I'm going to protect his sorry ass when they find out about those orders he shipped to Australia, he's sadly mistaken!
27) Eight o'clock *Star Trek* re-run, Lakers versus Celtics at nine—and then hello, Pay Per View!

28) Come on, Reverend, pick up the pace a bit! We're all dying here!
29) You know, I'll bet egg whites would make my pie crusts flakier.
30) Would anybody notice if I called Domino's and had a pizza delivered?
31) Ugh! She just blew her nose on that thing, and now he's putting it back in his pocket. That can't be healthy.
32) Did I leave the iron on?
33) Whoa! Did he just move!? He couldn't have moved, dummy. He's dead.
34) Has anybody else noticed that Windows has always been just a bad imitation of Macintosh?
35) Dadaists, Surrealists, Cubists ... I finally see how they all fit together.
36) I actually prefer the industrial-grade toilet paper. That fluffy stuff falls apart too easily.
37) What's up with that yellow carpet stain over there?
38) He was a jerk. I'll get more people than this at my funeral.
39) Finally! Let's eat!

Previous Lives

Karen and Robert's gift certificate for the fortune-teller was the oddest of their engagement gifts, but they had nothing better to do on a rainy Saturday afternoon.

Karen squeezed Robert's hand in anticipation as she asked Madame Snowberry between flips of her magical cards, "Did we know each other in a previous life?"

"Oh, we shall see!" Madame Snowberry's eyes widened as she turned the next card. "Why, yes! You two were very close in one of your past lives."

Robert chuckled through his skepticism, but he leaned deeper into Karen, who responded by angling her head against his shoulder.

"Were we soul mates?" Robert asked.

"We shall discover that as well," Madame Snowberry whispered, pausing to drag out the drama for just a few more seconds. She so wanted to give this nice, young couple a fun experience to talk about at their upcoming wedding.

When she flipped the next card, however, Madame Snowberry's smile twitched, and she stared at the mysterious paper rectangle on the table between her and the lovely young couple.

"Not soul mates, I'm afraid," she croaked.

"But you said we were close," Karen implored. She and Robert exchanged glances.

"Yes, you were—as close as two people can get," the fortune-teller replied. This was the least favorite part of her job, the curse buried within her gift. "But you were not *soul* mates."

She sighed and met their expectant gazes. "You were *cell* mates."

Gym Day

Rick tossed his workout towel at Ben to get his attention. Ben paused between repetition sets on the butterfly press.

"See her?" Rick whispered, flicking his eyes toward an athletic woman striding on the elliptical machine about twenty feet away. Ben nodded, sweat pooling on his nose. Rick bent down close to Ben's ear. "What do you think it would be like to do her?" he asked with a leer.

Ben thought of Rick's wife, Allison, right that minute working her second job keeping the books for a local landscaping business between trips hauling her and Rick's kids to various soccer games and piano lessons. Allison always had a smile and a kind word for Ben. She often suggested fixing him up with one of her friends. "Nice guy like you," she said. "They'd be lucky!"

Ben looked from the woman to Rick and replied, "It's probably almost exactly like being with Allison."

Rick stopped staring at the young woman on the elliptical and turned a sharp gaze toward Ben. "How do you figure?"

Ben started a new set of lifts, pounding the metal bars together with a resounding clank a foot in front of this face. "Because you don't love her either."

Thank You For Calling

"Thank you for calling the suicide prevention hotline. We're sorry, but no one is available to take your call. Please leave a message at the tone, and we'll get back to you as soon as possible ... *Beep.*"

Handsome Stranger

When Anne saw the remarkable stranger walking a dog in the park on an otherwise ordinary summer evening, she sensed that fate had arranged for this man to cross her path. Her mind could only hold one thought: *This is the most handsome man I have ever seen.*

"Hello," the handsome man said through a smile so white his teeth pulled light from the air around his mouth.

Anne could hardly believe he had spoken to her, had said the word "hello" through lips so full and perfectly shaped for kissing.

"Hello," she replied through her own lips, which were suddenly dry.

"I'm Paul," the handsome stranger said, his voice a mix of honey and cello. "I just moved in down the street."

"I'm Anne," she said, grasping handsome Paul's offered right hand, his big, soft hand that buried hers. His left hand, dangling from a thick wrist, well-muscled arm, and square shoulder, held the dog's leash. That lovely hand, Anne noticed, held no wedding ring.

"This is Bowser," handsome Paul said, nodding a square jaw darkened with thick evening whiskers toward the dog standing beside his sandaled feet.

Anne tore her eyes from Paul's handsomeness to look at the dog for the first time. Bowser was mid-sized, about two feet tall, the color of charcoal, so dusky he looked like he would darken the palms of anyone who touched him.

"Hi, Bowser," Anne said, noticing the affected lilt in her own voice. Anne wasn't a "dog person." She didn't have one as a child and had never felt the need for one as an adult. She had no interest in paying for, housing, feeding, walking, and cleaning up after such creatures. She could take them or leave them. In Anne's experience, humans made the best companions--humans like Paul, for example.

Handsome Paul was leashed to this dog at this moment, so this dog was worth the effort. Anne knelt beside Bowser, whom she now noticed was a mutt of undeterminable lineage--and not a good mix. Maybe some Lab, perhaps some dachshund, a pinch of boxer, a hint of terrier--overall, more a chunking of attributes than a true blend. He was as thick around as a beer keg with a football head, meatloaf neck, and short, spindly legs.

"I think Bowser likes you," handsome Paul said. "Don't you, Bowser?"

Bowser grunted and thrust his head at Anne. Reflexively, she put her hand on his back but had to consciously force herself not to pull away. Bowser's spine bones jutted into her palm through his wire coat. Dander dust wafted from just the light stroke she gave him.

It's not his fault, Anne thought. *He's a dog. He can't help being a little dirty. Think about how handsome Paul is. Just keep petting. Pet the dog. Think of Paul. Pet the dog. Think of Paul ... handsome, handsome Paul.*

"He likes being scratched behind the ears," handsome Paul said. Anne glanced up at him. She liked the view from this angle. *Yep,* she thought, *just as handsome as he was fifteen seconds ago.*

Anne looked down at the big ears on the back of Bowser's clunky head. The skin was scabrous. Anne thought of how Paul's wavy hair was nothing like Bowser's ratty rug. She guided her fingernails lightly over the ruined, patch-furred skin just behind Bowser's right ear.

Bowser looked up to meet Anne's gaze. His right eye was ink-dark and featureless. His left was circled in a blood-red, inside-out lid. That eye bulged, nearly disconnected from the socket. Bowser eased his snout closer to Anne's face. His breath smelled like something found months too late in the back of the refrigerator, something turned green with fur growing on it. Bowser's moldy tongue lulled across one side of his jaw. Anne saw only four intact teeth, and the holes in Bowser's gums oozed pink puss.

"Awww, he wants a kiss," handsome Paul cooed. "Bowser wants a kiss. Go ahead, Anne. Give Bowser a kiss."

At the sound of his handsome master's voice, Bowser licked the puss from his gums and dribbled a yellowish glob of phlegm to the ground. Anne had to pull her foot away to avoid the glob landing on her newly purchased walking shoes, a maneuver that nearly sent her toppling over.

Anne regained her balance and stood so quickly that Bowser and handsome Paul both backpedaled. "I just remembered something," she sputtered, striding down the sidewalk like a power-walker. "I have to be someplace for something," she called over her shoulder to Paul, his smile drooping like the sagging leash he held, like the slack skin at Bowser's four armpits.

Anne didn't look back at handsome Paul, couldn't look. She walked straight toward her echoing house--a house with no pets, no kids, no husband.

One thought filled her mind: *Nobody is that handsome.*

The Cows Discover Religion

As the blustering helicopter passes noisily above the pasture fields, four previously indifferent cows, unknowing and afraid, run to shelter beneath the shady maple trees. They hide there, panting but quiet in the artificial wind. Their sixteen black hooves push heavily into the surface of this modern world. Standing close, each one searches out the others' eyes. As the air grows calm, their breathing slows. They bow their heads and begin to sing.

Happy Holidays

When she was twelve, April's father was transporting the Easter ham from the outdoor grill to the kitchen and dropped it onto the breezeway's concrete floor. April's mother, of course, was furious. Moments later, both parents screamed at each other over the ruined meat. Pineapple glaze, April's favorite, oozed into the pores of that rough floor, built so many years ago by the original owner of their ancient farmhouse.

From that day forward, nothing was the same. Her parents' holiday arguments grew more common as the years passed, making fancy meals an endangered species in April's home. Thanksgiving drumsticks were wielded as clubs. The Christmas roast was lobbed like a grenade and left on the floor as luxurious dog food. Jellied cranberry sauce dripped from walls like Technicolor blood at the multiplex.

Now, so many years later, April has a family of her own. But she's more careful. Her family battles are fought on random weekdays over ordinary plates of fish sticks or peanut butter sandwiches or mac and cheese.

Her children will grow up with happy holidays.

Distance

Shawn looked forward to seeing Shannon, his favorite bank teller, every afternoon when he made his regular deposit. He could have used the drive-through or even the impersonal electronic banking, but he enjoyed seeing Shannon each day. She always smiled and spoke happily to him, even if the conversation was always a variation on the conversation of the day before. Lately, though, as she advanced into the eighth month of her pregnancy, Shannon seemed to grow more distant each day—figuratively and literally—although, when he considered the true depth of their relationship, maybe that was all in his imagination.

Signs of Intelligent Life

Scientists discovered the technology to observe the alien world so similar to our own back in the 1950s. Communication wasn't possible—only observation. The process was surprisingly simple: applying atomic energy to telescopic lenses and radio waves. Unfortunately, space flight was many decades behind the ability to watch, so meeting these cosmic neighbors wasn't yet possible. Instead, a team of government officials, scientists, philosophers, and educators studied every aspect of the intelligent life on that far-off planet for nearly a century while they simultaneously worked to build a ship to visit the new world.

During those many decades, the observers saw the planet's relatively primitive occupants gradually advance in significant ways, growing technologically, socially, morally, and artistically. Their progress wasn't perfect, and they suffered many setbacks, but they seemed destined to make their world into an advanced society with peace, cooperation, and equal opportunity, given enough time.

But then, just when the observers thought that the alien race might advance enough to make a compatible ally, disaster struck. Frightened and confused by their own progress, they let a leader emerge who represented their worst instincts and preyed upon their weaknesses to lead them down a path of hatred, xenophobia, and deceit. Following his example, the alien creatures eventually descended into bigotry, violence, environmental neglect, and, ultimately, a devastating world war that wiped out all living creatures in less than five years.

This distant tragedy took place only a few years before the observers banded together to complete their great craft for the trip across the gulf of space to the parallel planet. The sad irony was not lost on those who put away childish differences and saw that what united them was far greater than anything that could divide them. They had hoped to come together in peace with the beings on this new world. Sadly, that would never be. As they helplessly watched the other planet destroy itself, they vowed not to let the same fate befall their own existence.

When, at last, their ship landed on the strange planet, two crew members stepped out into the still-smoking remains of the ruined world. This place had once been so lush and full of life, but it was now something from a child's nightmare.

The travelers immediately went to a graveyard where the most intelligent beings on the planet went to die. The first crew member bent down and lifted a long, white bone from the dirt and held it aloft for her companion to see.

"I'm honored to hold what's left of a being so wise and dignified," she said.

"Yes," her crewmate replied. "They were majestic in every way."

The first crewmember held the bone out to the other. "If only these elephants had governed this world," she said with a sigh.

The second crewmember extended one of his three arms and gently lifted the elephant bone from the eight-fingered hand of his crewmate.

"If the elephants had led this world instead of those foolish humans," he mused while examining the bone with five of his seven eyes, "then perhaps there would still be intelligent life here on Earth to greet us."

Immigrant

Juan walked to his new job in the unfamiliar neighborhood with his eyes down, his hands pushed deep in his pockets. But then he thought he heard a voice calling his name, friendly and familiar, so he turned, smiled, searched hopefully down the long street—but saw only strangers' faces.

Not All Heroes Wear Capes

Nathan liked to leave his change in the vending machine because it was worth a few random coins to know that the next person who buys a candy bar will feel like a lottery winner for about five seconds.

Obit

He often bit his mother's nipple because he liked the taste of blood. He held his baby sister's head under the bath water long enough to know it was wrong. He often peed in the corner of his second-grade coatroom instead of walking the extra steps to the bathroom and only stopped doing it because he was afraid of getting caught. He broke a friend's finger with a well-aimed dodgeball throw and was happier about the skill of the throw than worried about his friend's finger. He blew his nose on the basketball towels he knew his teammates used to wipe their faces. He told the girl whose virginity he took that she was too ugly to take to the prom. He fantasized about killing the professor who gave him his only failing college grade but just slashed the guy's tires instead. He listed on his résumé three jobs, two awards, and a reference that didn't exist. He borrowed from petty cash four times but only returned the money once. He slept with a coworker two weeks after his wedding. He lied to charity solicitors that he gave to other projects. He started gossip about himself so that he could claim not to dignify it with a response. He got his last promotion with a promise to lay off as many people as possible. He went to Tea Party rallies and voted Republican but applied for stimulus funds. He loved Donald Trump because Trump hated the same people he did. He responded to his diagnosis at age forty-three by thinking about his new car before his children. He told his wife that his deathbed wish was for his funeral music to feature the Billy Joel classic, "Only the Good Die Young."

Patience

While taking down the Christmas lights, Roger paused to wipe a forearm across his face. "Damn," he muttered, steadying the ladder, "this is one hot July we're having this year."

The Jogger

Every morning around 10, he would jog a few hundred feet and then pull a comb from the waistband of his gym shorts and run it through his hair. That was his routine, every morning: jog a little, comb a lot, jog a little more, comb a lot more. He went around the block maybe three or four times, taking more and more time with his hair and less and less time jogging, sort of giving himself extended cool-down periods. He even jogged on weekends, sometimes getting funny looks from the folks mowing their lawns or raking leaves. He even jogged in the winter, wearing the same gym shorts and running shoes as he mucked his way through the unshoveled sidewalks.

He wasn't in very good shape, but, *damn*, that guy's hair looked *fantastic*.

Compound-Word Adjectives

If Gretchen had leaned one thing during fifteen weeks of Professor Madjek's Introduction to Creative Writing class, it was that no one could write without inspiration. And Professor Madjek could always provide her with just the right amount of inspiration.

"Okay," the professor said to the class. "This is our final meeting and our final in-class writing prompt. So I made it a good one. Here you go: Write a story that somehow touches on all of these elements: food, adultery, a newspaper, murder, and punctuation."

The other students groaned, but Gretchen opened her notebook and began right away. Her protagonist's name would be Lynnette. The food would be chili. The newspaper would be open to the sports section. The rest of the story? Well, she would figure out as she went along.

In blue ink on lined white paper, she wrote the words, *"We learned something really interesting in English class today ..."*

* * *

"We learned something really interesting in English class today," Lynnette told her husband Hugo over the crock-pot chili she had made for dinner. Now that they were an empty-nest couple, she started her fifth-decade years by taking classes at the local community college.

"Professor Madjek told us," she continued, "that compound-word adjectives are groups of two or more words that come directly before the noun they modify." She leaned toward Hugo and pulled down the corner of his sports section. "Here's the interesting part: You have to use a hyphen when the compound-word adjective comes *directly* before the noun, but *not* if it isn't directly before the noun."

Hugo looked up from the baseball box-score reports and stared at her.

"Yeah?" he said. "You think that's interesting? Is that the kind of useless-ass crap you're learning at that fancy-pants community college? I hated English in high school, and I got negative-zero interest in hearing about it now."

Lynnette dropped the corner of the paper, which floated down into Hugo's half-eaten bowl of chili. He didn't seem to notice the red-brown liquid slowly soaking into the porous newsprint.

"Here's another thing about that college," Hugo continued. "If your smarty-smart Professor Madjek knows so much, why ain't he teaching at the state university instead of misfit-toys community college for brain-damaged teenagers and washed-up, middle-aged housewives?"

Lynnette glared. "For your information, Professor Madjek is very smart. He used to teach at a university in the Midwest, but he likes community colleges better. He said it's a local-outreach thing for him. He can make the world a better place by providing learner-centered education in a nurture-based environment."

"Sounds like he missed his life-long calling," Hugo replied, wiping chili stains from the point-spread listings for this weekend's football games. "He ought to be a bleeding-heart nursemaid instead of a professor."

Lynnette grabbed Hugo's bowl and dropped it into the sink with her own. Despite the twenty-year gap with her older husband, Lynnette knew Hugo wasn't a hearing-impaired person. But he still failed to notice the nerve-jangling clang of the bowl in the stainless-steel sink as he kept talking in his cringe-inducing voice.

"You know what? Your precious Professor Madjek seems like a pansy-ass fruitcake, if you ask me. He spends his whole day running off at the mouth about adjectives and poetry—that sounds pretty queer-ball homo to me."

Lynnette rinsed the chili residue from the bowls and rubbed them hard with the scratchy soap pad. She resisted a near-overwhelming urge to break one of the bowls over Hugo's suitcase-sized head as he left the table, carrying the sports section to the upstairs bathroom for his usual half-hour, post-dinner session on the toilet.

While she dried her hands on the flower-bordered towel, she thought of how she rubbed those same hands over Professor Madjek's rock-hard abdominal muscles that afternoon in his office after class. He had kissed her with that heat-probing tongue of his that always made her head spin. Pansy-ass fruitcake? Lynnette chuckled. Queer-ball homo? Not hardly.

Then she thought of the new ingredient she had added to Hugo's chili just before she served it to him: *Detection-proof poison.*

* * *

When Gretchen wrote that final line, she looked up and realized that she was the last student left in the classroom.

"How's it going, Gretchen?" Professor Madjek asked. He had retired from full-time teaching a few years before, but he liked coming back to teach Introduction to Creative Writing each semester.

He rose from his desk chair where he had been reading the latest John Grisham novel. There was a time for the classics, and a time for a little excitement from the printed page. He suppressed a groan as his knee glitched and his back unfolded slowly. At seventy, he didn't get around quite as well as he used to, but he still had a twinkle in his eye and a passion for life.

Gretchen pulled her story from the notebook and slowly stripped away the fringe where the paper had come away from the spiral binding.

"This writing prompt really inspired me," she said, handing the pages to the professor as she moved toward the door.

"I'm glad," he said, thinking about how much he needed to use the bathroom after the long class. "You've done such great work this semester." He slid her story into the folder with the others and dropped it into his briefcase.

"By the way," Gretchen called from the door, "I'm sorry, but I won't be able to take your Advanced Creative Writing class next semester."

"Oh, that's too bad," Professor Madjek said. "I was really looking forward to working with you again." He patted the side of his well-used briefcase. "But I can't wait to read this one!"

Invitation

After their hike, Ed's wife Beth called from the upstairs bedroom, "Honey, can you come here, please? I'm naked."

Their marriage had settled into the routine of middle age lately, so Ed was thrilled with the invitation. Despite the ache in his knees after five miles on hilly trails, Ed took the stairs two at a time, bounding toward the love of his life.

As he entered their bedroom, Ed saw Beth seated on the edge of their bed, naked as promised.

"Can you check me for ticks before my shower?" she asked. "Gotta be careful these days. Thanks, honey."

Fabric

Dominic smoothed Michelle's cotton blouse across the ironing board. His hands moved slowly, tenderly, savoring the heat in the now-smooth fabric, the hiss of steam rising. The people who knew them well thought it was sweet that he still did her laundry after four decades of marriage. "What a cute, old couple!" he once overheard a neighbor say about them. As he placed the blouse on a hanger, Dominic revisited the memory of Michelle quickly unbuttoning that same blouse the night before, of her letting it fall in a wrinkled heap to the floor, her bare skin pressing hot against his.

Faking It

The call came at 7:30, exploding Jack from Saturday morning sleep. It was the admission director at the community college where Jack teaches.

"Monica was going to talk about careers in the liberal arts, but she called in sick. Twenty people signed up. It starts in half an hour. Can you do it?"

Jack agreed, silently cursed his colleague Monica, gobbled some toast, ducked in and out of the shower, dragged a toothbrush through his mouth, put on a necktie, and raced to the community college where he'd taught writing and communications for a decade.

This was a recruiting program to attract new students. They mainly came from the technical high schools in the area. These were kids who either didn't like or had trouble with the traditional academic program. They were the bread and butter, the ones who weren't going to big state universities or small, selective colleges. Open enrollment, minuscule tuition, and practical programs attracted them.

Today's event included introductions to such programs as accounting, computer repair, office administration, and machine technology, among the many other job-preparation areas of the curriculum. The "Careers in the Liberal Arts" session Jack was drafted to chair stood out like a sore thumb that also had a broken nail painted pink.

He had a hard time believing that twenty people would sign up for such an oxymoron. Perhaps they were late registrants closed out of the "real" sessions. Maybe they were just confused. Jack certainly was.

When he walked into the room, there were indeed twenty young people staring at him, waiting for him to enlighten them for the next hour. In the back corner sat two of their teachers in jeans and sweatshirts, looking as content as if they had just taken a break from tending their vegetable gardens to pop in for a visit.

Jack killed about ten minutes rambling about the college in general: small class size, great parking, and caring staff. Then he spent fifteen minutes trying to define the indefinite. Just what the hell is "liberal arts" anyway? He couldn't help thinking that his explanation only managed to confuse them (and himself) even more.

He asked them what careers they were interested in. One young man raised his hand and said, "H-VAC." Ignorance and embarrassment were now added to Jack's confusion when he had to ask him what "H-VAC" was. "Heating, ventilation, and air conditioning," the kid told him without a trace of condescension. No one else volunteered a career choice.

Another five minutes gone—although Jack honestly believed that the clock on the classroom wall actually started ticking backward.

Finally, Jack turned to what he knew best: writing, critical thinking, communications. "You'll all have to write reports for your jobs, give presentations to clients," he said. "Employers want people who can work together and think creatively, not just do what they're told."

That took ten minutes. Then he asked for their questions. "Sorry," Jack responded, "but we don't have any sports teams."

Jack let them go ten minutes before the hour was up. Giving them plenty of time to get to their next session was his excuse, but they knew he had nothing left to say. They gave him a smattering of polite applause before leaving anyway.

As everyone filed out, the two teachers beamed at Jack. They clapped his shoulders and pumped his hand, happy, it seemed, not to be the ones faking it for a change.

Status

Facebook Status: I kicked ass on my run around the reservoir this afternoon! The 90+ degree heat didn't bother me at all as I set a new personal-best time for this four-mile run! Age can't catch me! I run too fast! I'll be dancing at the clubs 'til midnight if anyone wants to try to keep up with me!

Reality Status: The heat was sort of bearable in the shade, but the bugs were so bad out of the sun that I think I sprained my elbow swatting them away from my face. I jogged at a 20-minute mile pace and walked almost half the time to avoid passing out. At one point, I was thinking, *If you pass out, try to fall straight ahead and not to the right into the water where you'd drown in five minutes or to the left into the thick brush where the rescue workers would never find you.* The wind kept knocking me backward and seemed to be in my face the whole way around, if that's even possible. My good knee is now my bad knee and my bad knee is my worse knee. My knee doctor is going to ask me if I know I'm in my fifties when I see him next week. My car is going to smell like fish for a month because I leaked a gallon of sweat into the seat on the drive back. I'm home now, having Tylenol and alcohol with my feet propped up in front of the air conditioner. I'm going to feel like crap tomorrow, but I guess I'm glad I did it. Please don't call or text tonight because I'll be in bed by seven.

One Thing

"There's one thing that always works," Marty said as he steered the car along the interstate. "One thing that always cheers me up if I'm feeling down."

He could feel Debbie looking at him from the passenger seat. They'd been dating for three months, and things seemed to be getting serious. There were no enormous "red flags"—just a few small ones, barely pale pink, nothing that they couldn't deal with.

"It's something dirty, right?" Debbie asked, not laughing. "Is it something dirty?"

"No," Marty said, chuckling. "Nothing dirty."

"What is it?" Debbie asked.

Marty inhaled and was about to answer, about to tell her that a simple hand on his shoulder was all he ever needed to feel better, when Debbie interrupted: "Wait! Don't tell me. It's too much pressure! I don't want you to be disappointed if I don't do it."

One far off day in some indefinite future, Marty's daughter or son would ask him, "How did you know you were really in love? How did you know you were with the right person?" And by then Marty would have found the right person because that's why he would have a daughter or son. Maybe by then he'd be able to answer his child's question. Maybe by then he'd know about finding the right person. Marty envied that future version of himself.

But for that moment, as Marty steered the car toward the freeway exit and Debbie changed the subject to whatever their plans might have been for that evening, the only question he could answer for certain was how he knew he was with the wrong person.

Spooning

Except for the occasional dinner outing or breakfast date, the two spoons had snuggled contentedly in the closed-drawer darkness for decades. Lately, though, they each felt the same vague longing—though each would never be able to voice it to the other: *It sure would be nice to fork once in a while.*

Ant Traps

On the first day in their new house, the young couple unpacked and kept marveling—such a big place at a reasonable price on a quiet street.

On the second day, they noticed the ants. Some were large, meaty things that seemed angered by the invasion of their home. Others were tiny, barely visible, and seemed unconcerned with the humans' arrival, probably because they outnumbered them several billion to two.

On the third day, they sought help at the hardware store.

"We need some ant traps," the wife said to the middle-aged man behind the counter. His smile faded, and he looked at her as if she had just threatened his dog.

"You can't get that here," the man said.

"You don't carry ant traps?" the husband asked.

The man seemed offended. "Of course not. I don't even think that's legal."

The husband began a response, sucked air into his lungs the way he did before swear words were about to surface, but his wife touched his arm.

"Well," she said, "We have ants in our new house. Do you know where we can get ant traps?"

The man stared at her for a long moment, and then he spat laughter.

"What the hell is so funny?" the husband asked.

"You want *ant traps*," the man said between chuckles. "I thought you were asking for *anthrax*."

By the tenth day, when the ants had actually carried away all of the ant traps, the young couple began to wonder if maybe anthrax would have worked better after all.

Child of the Decade Award Acceptance Speech, December 31, 1969

Thank you, ladies and gentlemen. It is with humility and gratitude that I accept this Child of the Decade Award. The 1960s were a turbulent time in our nation's history, a time when we all awakened to the possibilities of life beyond racism, sexism, and classism. I am very, very thankful that my small example as Child of the Decade contributed to this history-making era.

My journey began shortly after the Pittsburgh Pirates clinched the National League pennant in the fall of 1960. My heartfelt thanks go out to the Pirates' players, managers, and team officials for inspiring my father and mother to celebrate their achievement by conceiving me. The team's subsequent World Series victory helped to keep my parents' marriage happy and provided me with a stable home for years to come.

I would also like to thank my twin brother for his companionship during those gestational months together. Our telepathic conversations and shared memories of the origin of the human species were an endless source of encouragement, enlightenment, and delight. I can only hope that our time together contributed in some small way as he ascended to the presidency of his class at Winslow Elementary School, the youngest third-grader to hold such office.

The many teachers who have given of their time and energy to guide my education deserve so much more than my meager thank-yous. Without their support, my eighteen weeks of public school, six months of college, and two years for combined medical and legal degrees at Yale University would have taken much longer and delayed my path in life. We are all learners, but these people with great minds and hearts and spirits, I am proud to call my teachers.

I would be unforgivably remiss if I did not mention the many wonderful men and women of the Professional Bowlers Association who gladly granted me an age exception so that I could tour the great cities of America and pursue my passion for the pins. The championships I've won are nothing compared with the friendships I've made. Although it is not enough to show my gratitude, I would like to donate my $800,000 prize money from this year's tournaments to the Kegglers Against Cancer Fund.

To the editors of all the magazines, newspapers, and anthologies that have printed my early scrawlings, I send my thanks for your support and encouragement. To everyone at Doubleday who helped me realize a new dream with the publication of each of my seven novels, four short story collections, seven books of essays, and twelve volumes of poetry, and to the great people at Oxford University Press for championing my textbooks on physics, organic chemistry, prosody, and social theory—what words can I add other than, "Thank you so much"?

My appreciation also goes out to President Richard Nixon for inviting me to the White House so many times. You have often told me how much my counsel has meant to you as you perform the duties of your esteemed office, but I pray that I have shown a fraction of the guidance that you have provided me. While we may disagree on many policies and tactics, we always shared the best interests of humanity. I only wish we had kept some kind of recording of our many conversations on foreign and domestic policy to enlighten future generations.

Tomorrow, as I meet with leaders from around the globe at the World Conference on Peace and Prosperity for the 1970s, I will do everything that I can to live up to the honor bestowed upon me this evening. Perhaps if we can all come together and show one another the same care and commitment that my parents gave to me through these nearly nine wonderful years, the coming decade will indeed be one that brings the world together.

Thanks, Mom and Dad. I love you!

Horror Story

After a year of making hundreds of calls each day, wearing out another pair of shoes every few weeks, and knocking on more doors than he thought could exist in the whole country, David planned to take his family for a well-earned weekend in the country on the first Saturday of November.

As David watched the famous buildings of the capital city fade in his rearview mirror, he nicked a tiny patch of early morning ice and spun his car through the railing of the Virginia side of the Francis Scott Key Memorial Bridge. His wife and kids slipped through the windows before the car dipped beneath the water. They had only cuts, bruises, and a terrible scare.

But David had to be pulled from the Potomac River's chilly water by the strong hands of a local fisherman who happened to be a former college swimmer. His plunge sent him into a coma that lasted for two long months in a sad wing of the city's largest hospital.

When he unexpectedly awoke, the medical staff sprinted from the room's television, clicking off a shouting match on a news program that David couldn't quite hear. Dark expressions hovered above the lab coats crowded around his bed.

"I'm alive?" David asked.

The faces nodded but remained troubled. David grimaced, swallowed hard on his arid throat.

"My wife?" he croaked. "My children?"

"They're fine," the nurse told him, expelling a held breath. She encouraged him to drink slowly from a small plastic cup. The icy water burned.

"Why?" he asked between painful sips. "Why do you all look so terrified?"

"We have some ..." The head physician halted. His gaze found the floor.

The nurse rescued his sentence: "... some horrible news."

She inhaled a long, slow, deep breath of filtered hospital air and spoke two hushed words: "Trump won."

David's screams could be heard all the way to Pennsylvania Avenue.

The First Day of College Classes, Fall Semester, 2036

"Good morning, everyone," the professor said looking out at the enthusiastic room full of vibrant young people. She pulled up a class roster on her palm-sized tablet. "When I call your first name, please raise your hand. Okay? First up is Ashley."

"Here," a woman in the back row called out.

"Donald?"

"I go by Danald," a male student said quietly.

"Understandable," the professor replied. "Pence?"

A woman in the front row raised her hand. "I just had it legally changed to 'Hillary.'"

"Hillary?" the professor asked.

Five young women scattered around the classroom raised their hands and simultaneously said, "Here!"

"Oh, my!" The professor laughed. "We'll have to sort that one out later, maybe assign nicknames."

The whole class chuckled.

"Donalda?"

"Just 'D,' please," another woman said sharply, eyes fixed on the sunshine outside the window.

"Flynn?"

"I prefer to be called 'Duckworth,' ma'am," said an ROTC student in fatigues.

"Eric?"

A burly, white football player responded with a southern drawl, "I go by 'Barack.'"

The professor squinted and stuttered the next name: "Ja ... Jar ... Jarvanka?" There were audible gasps from around the room.

"Call me Michelle, please," said a student with a strong, clear voice. "Yes, I hate my parents." The gasps turned to chuckles.

"I think we're all with you on that one," the professor said.

Then she paused for a brief but noticeable instant before calling the next name. "Wall?"

"Yeah, I prefer 'Wally,'" a soft-voiced man said from the back corner.

"Wally it is," the professor repeated. "Good work making lemons into lemonade."

The professor hesitated again, brought the tablet closer to her face, shrugged. "Is this a misprint? Maga? M-A-G-A?"

"I'm transitioning to 'Maggie,'" said a tall, attractive woman.

"Congratulations!" the professor beamed. "Tweet?"

"Please call me 'Instagram,'" a stylishly dressed man replied, tapping his oversized smartwatch.

"Budi ... Budda ... Buja ..."

"Buttigieg," called out a bright, optimistic student who looked too young to be in college.

"Sashamalia?"

"Here!" came the energetic reply.

"All right, thanks everyone. I'm glad we have that out of the way," the professor said, tapping a set of controls on the instructor's console. "Let's begin the course. My name is Professor Reagan Bush-George, but please call me by my initials: RBG. Welcome to Political Science 200: Chaos to Enlightenment, 2016-2020."

The lights dimmed slightly, and a hologram appeared at the front of the classroom, slowly rotating for a 360-view. It depicted a life-sized man slouching in a shabby black suit and oversized red tie. His ruddy face was caught in deep grimace beneath a ridiculous flop of unnatural hair. The students recoiled an almost imperceptive degree as if they subconsciously sensed toxic radiation.

Hovering near the holograph were internet headlines reading, "Improbable Electoral College Victory," "Record Low Approvals," "Foreign Collusion," "Impeachment Debate," "Ousted in Historic Landslide," "Multiple Counts of Obstruction of Justice," and "First President Jailed After Leaving Office."

When the hologram pivoted to reveal the man's back, the students saw that his wrists were restrained by handcuffs. They relaxed their stiffened backs slightly and nodded in satisfaction.

The students powered up their touch-screen desks, synched them with their hand-held devices, and focused their attention on Professor RBG's words. After class, they'd do what college students have done since college began: meet up with friends, discover the best places to hang out, blow off energy, have conversations that would pivot from deep to shallow in an instant, possibly drink too much, perhaps even begin a fun but meaningless relationship.

But for this moment, they were all determined to learn everything they could to avoid the mistakes of the past and help create a better world in the future—especially the Hillarys.

Keeping Up

Once again, the golden glow of fall had turned into bare-branched winter in the Smith family's suburban neighborhood. As they did every year at this time, the Smiths looked forward to another season of measuring their life by making comparisons with what they saw through the neighboring Jones's bedroom window.

In a Jam

Max entered the dark photocopy room an hour before the office opened. He needed twenty copies of his résumé because he had a vague sense that things weren't going well for him at Bendix Corporation after his first-year evaluation.

To his frustration, all six copiers were jammed, so Max opened the nearest one, reached deep into its mechanical innards, and extracted a mangled sheet of paper. Smoothing it, he saw that it was a draft of his supervisor's evaluation report.

After a quick scan, Max pressed the reset button. *I'm gonna need a few hundred copies,* he thought. *At least.*

Change is Good?

Heidi sat in her favorite overstuffed reading chair in the early light of a Sunday morning at home. Marshall peeked over her shoulder to see her cell phone. Their bad-tempered cat, Blix, perched just behind Heidi's head atop the chair back, blocking Marshall's view of her phone.

Heidi wasn't reading today—just clutching that damned phone six inches from her nose.

"Finished your book for book group?" Marshall asked, sauntering behind her chair to try for a better view of her phone while pretending to look out the window into the back yard. Blix's head pivoted nearly 360 degrees to follow his path.

Heidi drew the phone down almost imperceptibly, tilted it just a few degrees away from his line of vision.

"Yesterday," Heidi replied. Marshall hadn't noticed her reading yesterday, something she usually did most of Saturday afternoon. He couldn't actually remember what they did yesterday afternoon. *A movie? No. Walk? No. Late lunch? No.*

Blix wasn't really bad-tempered. The cat just didn't seem to like Marshall, instead preferring to snuggle near Heidi's head on the chair back and stare at him. *Judgmentally?* Marshall wondered. *Maybe.*

As Marshall lingered behind the chair, Heidi's phone emitted the tiny whoosh of a text message launching into the mysterious world of cyberspace. Marshall never texted. He couldn't remember seeing Heidi text before either.

Marshall craned his neck to see Heidi's phone screen. When she got that phone a year ago, she had taken a photo of Marshall and installed it as her background photo. She said she liked the blank look on his face. "Not smiling, not frowning," she said at the time. "Just being you."

Marshall thought about how Heidi carried his image close to her in her purse—or, better yet, in her pocket, thin layers of fabric between his face on the phone screen and her bare skin.

Heidi's thumb swiped deftly across the phone screen, and the text evaporated just before Marshall could focus his eyes on the tiny words there. He recognized the homescreen with her icons arranged into all four corners of the glowing surface. But his face had been replaced. Instead, there was a photo of Blix spread across that same chair back.

"Why is Blix on your phone instead of me?" Marshall asked.

"Hmm?" Heidi murmured. "Oh, no reason. Sometimes change is good. You know?"

Marshall didn't know.

Blix stared at Marshall simultaneously from the image on the phone screen and in three dimensions from the back of her chair.

Then Heidi held the phone's power button down until everything went dark.

Double-Shift

Smitty was scheduled to work a double-shift that day—fifteen straight hours—so he chugged three bottles of Five Hour Energy drink. Did it work? No one knows yet because the Bureau of Missing Persons is still looking for him.

My Little Eye

The minivan consumed interstate highway miles like a swarm of locust defoliating a forest.

Little Eliza's eyes darted to every surface she could see from her raised safety seat. "I spy with my little eye," she said with all the anticipation a six-year-old could muster, "somethiiiinnnngggg ... black!"

"The cows?" Eliza's twin brother Elliot shouted from his matching safety seat, pointing out the window.

"No!" Eliza said.

"Daddy's glasses?" asked Eliza's mother Donna, not taking her tiring, forty-something eyes from the road or her hands from the proper ten-and-two position on the steering wheel.

"No!" Eliza said.

"Is it inside the car or outside?" Eliza's father Bud asked, cocking his head from the passenger seat.

"Inside!" Eliza called out gleefully.

"The back of the seat?" Elliot asked.

"No!" Eliza answered.

"Mommy's underpants?" Bud called out.

"Gross!" Elliot spurted.

"No, silly Daddy!" Eliza shouted.

The minivan flitted with guesses from person to person, some serious attempts to read Eliza's developing mind, some just words tossed out to fill the empty time and vacant space. Every guess was wrong. Eventually, a silence grew, not quite awkward. By then, awkward had become the background ambiance after the dozen hours since the drive began.

The highway ticked by beneath the rushing tires for a long moment, but then a voice rose from the third row of seats behind the twins. It was barely audible above the sudden staccato insect-buzz emanating from the earbuds that fifteen-year-old Zack had just removed with a jerk of his clenched fist as if he were pulling the ripcord on a parachute that failed to open miles above enemy territory on a moonless night.

"Is it the vast, echoing, well of emptiness where my soul should be?" Zack asked, his eyes staring through a shapeless smudge obscuring the pastoral landscape outside the window.

"No!" Eliza responded with a giggle.

"I give up," Donna said, not for the first time on the trip from New Jersey to their new life in rural Ohio.

"It's the steering wheel!" Eliza shouted.

"Ahhh!" said the whole family—even Zack.

Work Like a Dog

Dogs never punch a time clock. Dogs chew on time clocks. Dogs never hang their heads on a Sunday afternoon dreading the Monday morning return to work. Dogs soak in the sunshine on Sunday afternoon. Dogs never set their alarm clocks for 6 a.m. Dogs are unalarmed. Dogs never straighten their necktie for an important meeting. Dogs only wear a necktie for ironic photos on social media. Dogs never feel guilty about napping on company time. Dogs never get passed over for promotion. Dogs aren't mandated to take workshops on dealing with difficult coworkers. Dogs consent to their coworkers' sniffs and nuzzles. Dogs never have their lunch stolen from the office fridge. Dogs never lose sleep worrying about what the boss thinks. Dogs are the boss. Dogs never have to update their résumé. All dogs are qualified for all dog jobs. Dogs don't have to save for retirement. Dogs retire to Granddad's farm upstate. Dogs never bring work home. Dogs never miss their pup's fun and games while staying late at the office. Dogs don't care about the joy of leaving work for a two-week vacation. Dogs are on permanent two-week vacations. Dogs don't worry about their benefits package. Dogs are the benefits package. Dogs never let their inboxes get full. Dogs just let their toy boxes get full. Dogs don't check e-mail. Dogs check pee-mail. Dogs don't have to worry about "following their passion." Dogs are passion. Dogs don't need a lot of time for lunch. Dogs munch and go. Dogs don't need a break room. Every room is a dog's break room. Dogs never need to upgrade their software. Dogs don't worry about what they want to be when they grow up. Dogs don't grow up. Dogs don't need an office with a window. Any window could be a dog's office. Dogs don't TGIF. Every dog day is a Friday. Dogs don't take snow days. Dogs look forward to their performance evaluations. Dogs' staff meetings are way more fun than human staff meetings. Dogs work naked.

Winter Treat

When you're out walking your dog on a finger-numbing, tendon-tightening winter day, and she squats to pooh, as dogs have done since time began, and you coo to her, "good dog," you coo, "such a very good dog," as humans have also done since time began, because you're not just making noise, because she really is such a good dog, and you risk frostbite to take off a single glove and lick a fingertip to get the wet-finger adhesion you need to open the plastic poopie-bag, and then you thrust that icicle-fingered hand into the pocket of your heaviest coat, and you discover something small and round and hard, a hidden treasure you forgot was even there, and it's a doggie treat that's been hibernating within that lint-lined kingdom since at least the first true chilly day last fall when you practiced for the thousandth time "sit" and "wait" and "come," those classic greatest hits, just to keep you both in practice, and your dog somehow knows by nose-twitching instinct that your frozen paw is cradling a thing that used to be a treat, and you bend your frozen back to offer this desiccated little chunk of meat cereal, without demanding trick or obedience, just because you love-love-love her, and as she's crunching on what to her must be delicious, she looks up at you with those kindly space alien eyes that seem to broadcast directly to your warmest places, "I always knew you loved me, even without this treat," and you could swear her message includes the words, "I've always thought that you're a good dog too," before she buries her nose into the plow-tossed dirty snow while her still-fresh poop pulses welcome warmth into your bare hand through the tissue-thin poopie-bag, and the sun parts the clouds for the first time in what seems like years upon years upon years as this crazy winter that began before time began drags on and on, but you don't care because you know a dog who isn't so human that she might hide the fact that she loves you too, stale treat or no stale treat.

His First Mistake

After laboring for three quarters of a year, every impulse of his being told him that the time had come. He was prepared. He was on his way out. The world awaited him. His turn to make his way into the mysterious open air of the outside world had arrived. Making the decision that would define his life, he turned to his twin in the womb and said, "No, please, I insist. *You go first.*"

Question

Simon had never filled out a psychological survey at a job interview before. *First time for everything,* he thought.

Question seventeen asked, "Would you like to lose ten pounds even if it meant you'd be physically ill for a week?"

What a stupid question! Simon thought. But he needed a job, so he pretended to think deeply for the benefit of whoever was watching through the two-way mirror in the back of the conference room.

Simon meticulously darkened the circle with his #2 lead pencil. *What kind of a weirdo would rather be fat and feel good than sick and skinny?*

New Friends

Tom eased to a stop at the traffic light just behind a "short bus"—the kind that usually carries children with "special needs." One of the kids in the back seat turned to look out the rear window. The kid's expression seemed blank and distant. Tom knew these kids are often teased or ridiculed or just ignored, so he wanted to be friendly. He lifted a hand, waved, and smiled.

The kid's face instantly transformed into a smile, and Tom noticed that the boy was older than he had originally thought—maybe high school age. The kid waved back. Then he turned to the other kids on the bus and motioned for them to come to his window.

Tom was surprised to see that all the kids on the bus were male and at least as old as the first one. In fact, most of them looked like they could use a shave with a fresh blade.

And they all waved enthusiastically, maybe even a bit manically.

Tom noticed then that this bus wasn't the bright yellow usually associated with school children. It was a dull gray—putty would be a good word for it. That word could also describe the identical uniforms worn by all the guys in the bus.

About eight or nine of them crowded around the back windows, waving and laughing. The traffic light stayed stubbornly red for a long moment. Tom stopped waving and just sort of stared at the kids, trying to figure out what exactly was happening.

Then a couple of them started shaking their fists. A few more gave Tom the finger. One of them made a gesture Tom didn't understand that involved moving his curled hand to and from his open mouth and pushing his tongue against the inside of his cheek. Tom didn't like the look of things. He checked to make sure his doors were locked. He gripped the gearshift. He pretended to fiddle with the radio even though it wasn't on.

At last, the light changed. The bus was turning right, the same direction Tom needed to turn to go home. Instead, he continued on straight through the intersection even though that meant going five minutes out of his way to get back on the right track.

As the bus turned, Tom ventured one last glance. The guys had apparently lost interest, and he could see them turning away. Tom caught just a glimpse of the brown lettering on the gray side of the bus before it passed from view. It said "Dunlow." *What the hell is "Dunlow"?* Tom wondered.

But then it hit him. "Dunlow" is the name of the prison on the outskirts of town.

Sign

Jessica eased the car to a stop at the traffic light. She and Wayne had never been in this part of town before. The GPS told them that they were just a few minutes away from the new restaurant where they were meeting friends for dinner.

"What the hell?" Wayne said suddenly.

"What is it?" Jessica asked, following his gaze out the passenger window.

"Who would give something *that name?*" Wayne asked.

"Where?" Jessica said as she focused on a large sign between two bushes. *"Oh!"*

In big, brown, capital letters on a beige background, the sign read, ANAL PLACE.

"That can't be real," Wayne said.

"Must be some kind of joke," Jessica replied.

From the car behind them, someone tapped the horn, a polite reminder that the light had changed to green. Jessica and Wayne both kept their eyes on the sign while she inched the car forward. As their perspective changed, they saw the letters move out from behind the bush on the left.

"Ahhh!" they both said as Jessica fed the car more gas, and they sped on toward the restaurant.

"I think the waterfront is over that way," Jessica said.

"I guess there's a canal around here somewhere," Wayne replied.

"Yeah," Jessica said. "And we'll have a good story to tell at dinner."

Santa Nears Retirement

When Erin's son Charlie sat on Santa's knee at the mall in mid-December, Charlie asked Santa to get him a TIE Fighter from the new *Star Wars* movie for Christmas. Santa roared with approval and promised to get Charlie not only a typewriter, but some paper for it as well.

Dog Attack

This morning when Dustin was out walking his beagle, Princess, the darned little thing started to talk bad about Dustin's wife. One minute she was tugging on the leash and rooting in the dirt and pooping on the sidewalk like a normal dog, and the next she turned around and glared up at him and started ranting.

"I've got something to say, and you just better listen, mister," she growled in her throaty dog voice. "Just yesterday her highness neglected to give me a treat when I did that stupid trick she's always begging for. And she hasn't taken me for a walk in weeks. Can she get off her big butt and cut the web surfing down to five hours a day? And I'm not even going to mention the blanket in my crate. Pee-yew! Doesn't she know how the washing machine works? I gotta tell you man, how you put up with her, I have no idea."

"Hey, that's not fair, and you know it!" Dustin shouted, caught off guard by this tirade.

But by then Princess was pretending to be fascinated by a squirrel scampering up a nearby tree. A young couple pushing a baby carriage gave Dustin a strange look and hurried by, keeping as much of the sidewalk between themselves and Dustin as they could.

Dustin yanked the leash, pulling Princess away from the squirrel, and they resumed walking—but the walk was no longer fun for either of them. A great deal of unspoken tension hung in the air all the way home.

When they arrived at the back door, they could hear Dustin's wife moving around in the living room. As Dustin unhooked the leash from Princess's collar, he bent close to Princess's big stupid floppy ears and whispered with as much dignity as he could project, "We'll discuss this later."

What to do When the Neighbors' Dogs Won't Stop Barking for Thirty-Seven Nights in a Row

1) Call the "will do odd jobs" guy whose number you found on the bulletin board at the supermarket. Offer him twenty bucks. He'll know what to do.
2) Turn up the Republican National Convention really loud on the television. (This strategy won't shut up the dogs, but it will give you a new appreciation for their barking as a comparative source of intelligence in the world.)
3) Picture yourself at a peaceful beach being caressed by tranquil breezes and bathed in healing sunshine. Now picture the dogs at that same beach being chased by angry alligators.
4) Get one of those bulky suits worn by the people who train attack dogs. Smear the suit with bacon grease, put it on, and then let the dogs chew on you until they are too exhausted to bark anymore.
5) March right up to those dogs and tell them in a stern voice, "Cut it out you guys, and I mean right now!"
6) Invent a soundproof fence. Install it in the appropriate location.
7) Capture your other neighbor's cat and feed it to the dogs. (This is not actually recommended, but it crosses one's mind every now and then.)
8) Go on the Internet and see if you can find one of those dog whistles everybody seemed to have when you were a kid. What the heck—anything's worth a shot.

9) Place a personal ad on one of those internet dating websites. Play up the point that you are looking for someone who really, really likes dogs. (This is not recommended if you are married or in a serious, committed relationship.)
10) Tie an anonymous note to a brick and toss it through your neighbor's window. The note should say that you "know what they're up to" and "it had better stop really soon, or there might be more bricks." (Don't mention the dogs because that would be too obvious.)
11) Get some sleeping pills and some water. Bring the water to a vigorous boil. Add five pills. Add a bouillon cube (beef or chicken—your choice). Reduce heat to medium. Cover and let simmer for half an hour. Serve at room temperature in a doggie dish.
12) Call the neighbors pretending to be the police. Tell them there's been a rash of backyard dog abductions. Advise them to keep their dogs inside for at least a year.
13) When the dogs finally stop barking and fall asleep around 4:30 a.m., tiptoe up to them and yell, "It's about freaking time!"
14) Go to the pet store and purchase a large bucket of "Bark-Be-Gone." Apply liberally.
15) Ignore them. They'll stop ... yeah, just like that bully in junior high.
16) Eat lots of vegetables, exercise, take your vitamins, and outlive the hairy beasts by sixty years.
17) They say that living well is the best revenge, so buy a ten-year-old Chevy, drink wine that has a screw cap instead of a cork, and take a vacation to Dollywood.

18) Enroll in that community college continuing education course about dog mind control that you've always wanted to take but couldn't quite fit into your schedule.
19) Walk by the windows naked every few minutes. That should confuse them into silence.
20) Go to the library and check out a book about dog behavior. Make sure it's a big hardback. Throw it at them. Throw it hard.
21) Radio their coordinates to central command.
22) Read the dogs that notebook full of love poems you wrote in tenth grade.
23) Throw the dogs a surprise birthday party. Get a poodle in a bikini to jump out of a cake.
24) Become friends with the neighborhood kid who's really good with his slingshot. Invite him over for target practice.
25) Take up the tuba. Practice late at night in the part of your yard closest to your neighbors' bedroom window.
26) Move. Now.
27) When your neighbor comes out on the porch at midnight and says, "Will my sweet puppies please stop their barkie-warkies? Who're my good boys? Yes, you are, yes, you're my good boys, yes, you are, oh, my pookie-wookie puppies!" do a cell phone video of the whole thing. Make sure your lawyer gets the video into evidence at your trial. No jury would convict you.
28) Take comfort in the fact that only *cats* have nine lives.
29) Enter your neighbors in one of those "win-a-year-long-vacation-to-Madagascar" contests at the local

mall. Make sure it's the one that allows the winners to bring pets.
30) Join a support group. Confront your feelings. Get in touch with your inner child. Make peace with your demons. Tame your gremlin. Don't be afraid to cry.
31) Contact that horse whisperer guy. Ask him if he does dogs.
32) Begin a novel with the line, "It was a dark and stormy night, and my neighbors' dogs were barking again." Then secure a high-powered literary agent to handle this can't-miss bestseller.
33) Write a complaint letter to former President Bush. If anyone can help with such a difficult diplomatic situation, it's "W."
34) Mark your territory. You know what this means, and so will the dogs.
35) Help the dogs open a dot.com business. That should make them disappear pretty quickly.
36) Knit each dog a really nice sweater—maybe some booties and scarves as well. They've probably been trying to tell you that they're a little chilly.
37) Bark right back at the smelly bastards and see how they like it.

Made in the USA
Lexington, KY
04 November 2019